PERCY RUNS AWAY

by

The Rev. W. Awdry

with illustrations by
C. Reginald Dalby

Grolier

Percy Runs Away

HENRY, Gordon and James were shut up for several days. At last the Fat Controller opened the shed.

"I hope you are sorry," he said sternly, "and understand you are not so important after all. Thomas, Edward and Percy have worked the line very nicely. They need a change, and I will let you out if you promise to be good."

"Yes, Sir!" said the three engines, "we will."

"That's right, but please remember that this 'no shunting' nonsense must stop."

He told Edward, Thomas and Percy that they could go and play on the branch line for a few days.

They ran off happily and found Annie and Clarabel at the Junction. The two coaches were so pleased to see Thomas again, and he took them for a run at once. Edward and Percy played with trucks.

"Stop! Stop! Stop!" screamed the trucks as they were pushed into their proper sidings, but the two engines laughed and went on shunting till the trucks were tidily arranged.

Next, Edward took some empty trucks to the Quarry, and Percy was left alone.

Percy didn't mind that a bit; he liked watching trains and being cheeky to the engines.

"Hurry! Hurry! Hurry!" he would call to them. Gordon, Henry and James got very cross!

After a while he took some trucks over the main line to another siding. When they were tidy, he ran on to the main line again, and waited for the signalman to set the points so that he could cross back to the yard.

Edward had warned Percy: "Be careful on the Main Line; whistle to tell the signalman you are there."

But Percy didn't remember to whistle, and the signalman was so busy, and forgot Percy.

Bells rang in the signal-box; the man answered, saying the line was clear, and set the signals for the next train.

Percy waited and waited; the points were still against him. He looked along the main line . . . "Peep! Peep!" he whistled in horror for, rushing straight towards him, was Gordon with the Express.

"Poop poop poop poo-poo-poop!" whistled Gordon. His driver shut off steam and applied the brakes.

Percy's driver turned on full steam. "Back Percy! Back!" he urged; but Percy's wheels wouldn't turn quickly. Gordon was coming so fast that it seemed he couldn't stop. With shut eyes Percy waited for the crash. His driver and fireman jumped out.

"Oo—ooh e—er!" groaned Gordon. "Get out of my way."

Percy opened his eyes; Gordon had stopped with Percy's buffers a few inches from his own.

But Percy had begun to move. "I—won't stay—here—I'll—run—a—way," he puffed. He was soon clear of the station and running as fast as he could. He went through Edward's station whistling loudly, and was so frightened that he ran right up Gordon's hill without stopping.

He was tired then, and wanted to stop, but he couldn't . . . he had no driver to shut off steam and to apply the brakes.

"I shall have to run till my wheels wear out," he thought sadly. "Oh, dear! Oh, dear!"

"I—want—to—stop, I—want—to—stop," he puffed in a tired sort of way.

He passed another signal-box. "I know just what you want, little Percy," called the man kindly. He set the points, and Percy puffed wearily on to a nice empty siding ending in a big bank of earth.

Percy was too tired now to care where he went. "I—want—to—stop, I—want—to—stop—I—*have*—stopped!" he puffed thankfully, as his bunker buried itself in the bank.

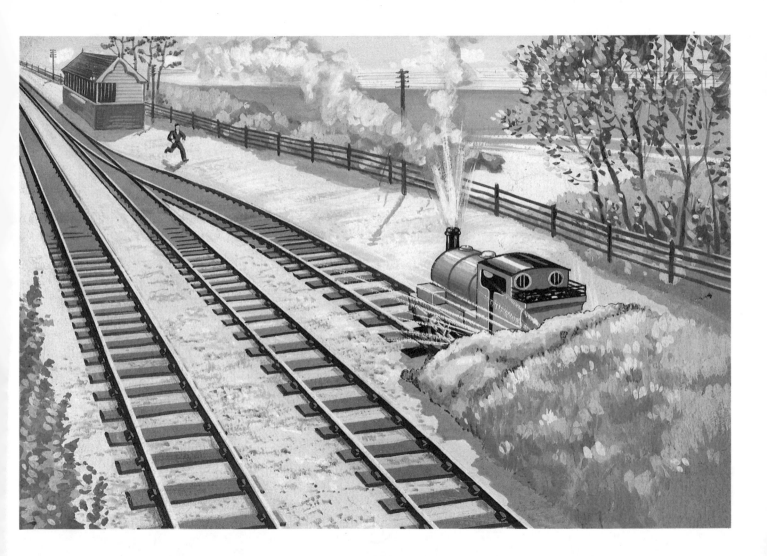

"Never mind, Percy," said the workmen as they dug him out, "you shall have a drink and some coal, and then you'll feel better."

Presently Gordon arrived.

"Well done, Percy, you started so quickly that you stopped a nasty accident."

"I'm sorry I was cheeky," said Percy, "you were clever to stop."

Percy now works in the yard and finds coaches for the trains. He is still cheeky because he is that sort of engine, but he is always *most* careful when he goes on the Main Line.

Percy's Promise

A MOB of excited children poured out of Annie and Clarabel one morning, and raced down to the beach.

"They're the Vicar's Sunday School," explained Thomas. "I'm busy this evening, but the Station-Master says I can ask you to take them home."

"Of course I will," promised Percy.

The children had a lovely day. But at tea-time it got very hot. Dark clouds loomed overhead. Then came lightning, thunder, and rain. The children only just managed to reach shelter before the deluge began.

Annie and Clarabel stood at the platform. The children scrambled in.

"Can we go home please, Station-Master?" asked the Vicar.

The Station-Master called Percy. "Take the children home quickly, please," he ordered.

The rain streamed down on Percy's boiler. "Ugh!" he shivered, and thought of his nice dry shed. Then he remembered.

"A promise is a promise," he told himself, "so here goes."

His driver was anxious. The river was rising fast. It foamed and swirled fiercely, threatening to flood the country any minute.

The rain beat in Percy's face. "I wish I could see, I wish I could see," he complained.

They left a cutting, and found themselves in water. "Oooh, my wheels!" shivered Percy. "It's cold!" but he struggled on.

"Ooooooooooooooooshshshshshsh!" he hissed, "it's sloshing my fire."

They stopped and backed the coaches to the cutting and waited while the guard found a telephone.

He returned looking gloomy.

"We couldn't go back if we wanted," he said, "the bridge near the Junction is down."

The fireman went to the guard's van carrying a hatchet.

"Hullo!" said the guard, "you look fierce."

"I want some dry wood for Percy's fire, please."

They broke up some boxes, but that did not satisfy the fireman. "I'll have some of your floor boards," he said.

"What! my nice floor," grumbled the guard. "I only swept it this morning," but he found a hatchet and helped.

Soon they had plenty of wood stored in Percy's bunker. His fire burnt well now. He felt warm and comfortable again.

"Buzzzzzzzzzzzzzzzz! Buzzzzzzzzzzzzzzzz! Buzzzzzzzzzzzzzzzz!"

"Oh, dear!" thought Percy sadly, "Harold helicopter's come to laugh at me."

Bump! something thudded on Percy's boiler. "Ow!" he exclaimed in a muffled voice, "that's really too bad! He needn't *throw* things."

His driver unwound a parachute from Percy's indignant front.

"Harold isn't throwing things at you," he laughed, "he's dropping hot drinks for us."

They all had a drink of cocoa, and felt better.

Percy had steam up now. "Peep peep! Thank you, Harold!" he whistled. "Come on, let's go."

The water lapped his wheels. "Ugh!" he shivered. It crept up and up and up. It reached his ash-pan, then it sloshed at his fire. "Ooooooooooooooooshshshshshshshshshshshsh!"

Percy was losing steam; but he plunged bravely on. "I promised," he panted, "I promised."

They piled his fire high with wood, and managed to keep him steaming.

"I *must* do it," he gasped, "I must, I must, I must."

He made a last great effort, and stood, exhausted but triumphant, on rails which were clear of the flood.

He rested to get steam back, then brought the train home.

"Three cheers for Percy!" called the Vicar, and the children nearly raised the roof!

The Fat Controller arrived in Harold. First he thanked the men. "Harold told me you were—er—wizard, Percy. He says he can beat you at some things . . ."

Percy snorted.

". . . but *not* at being a submarine." He chuckled. "I don't know what you've both been playing at, and I won't ask! But I do know that you're a Really Useful Engine."

"Oh, sir!" whispered Percy happily.